This book belongs to:

Sweet Dreams

Disney's Out & About With Pooh
A Grow and Learn Library

Published by Advance Publishers
© 1996 Disney Enterprises, Inc.
Based on the Pooh stories by A. A. Milne © The Pooh Properties Trust.

Written by Ronald Kidd
Illustrated by Arkadia Illustration Ltd.
Designed by Vickey Bolling
Produced by Bumpy Slide Books

ISBN:1-885222-63-7
10 9 8 7 6 5 4 3 2

Winnie the Pooh was looking at the most beautiful thing in the whole world. It was more beautiful than the trees or the clouds or a sunset over the pond.

He was looking into a pot full of honey.

Pooh gazed at it, smiling. He imagined all the wonderful times he and the honey were going to have. Then, suddenly, his smile faded.

What if it weren't really honey?

It looked like honey. It felt like honey. It sloshed in the pot like honey. But what if it were something very different? Pooh knew there was just one way to find out. Someone would have to taste it — and so he did.

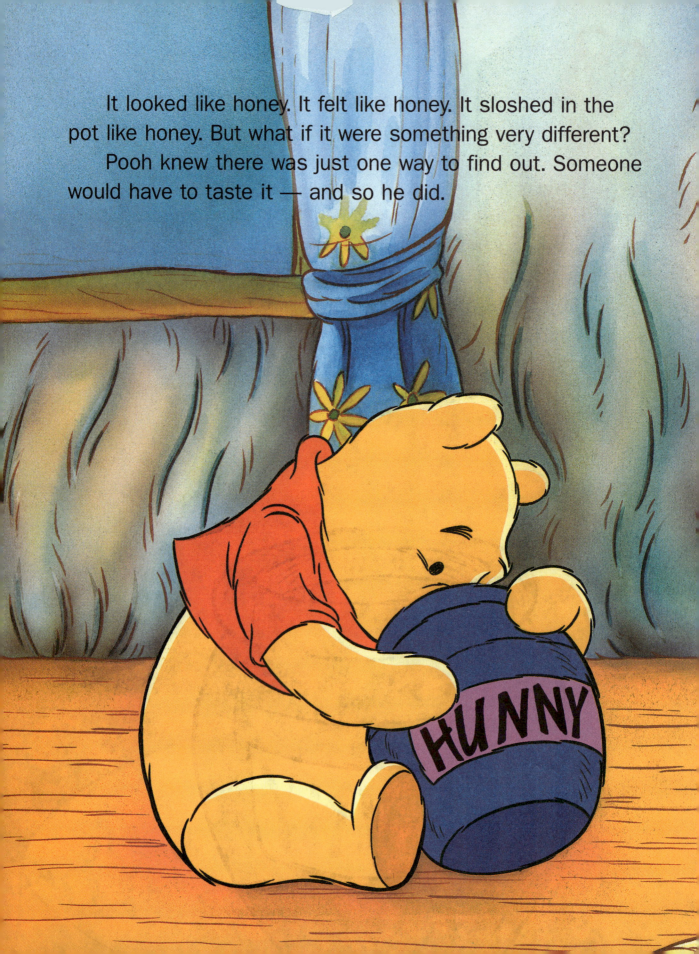

When Pooh looked up a bit later, Piglet was standing there.

"Hello, Piglet," said Pooh. "I'm happy to say that this pot is full of real honey."

Piglet looked into the pot. "Pooh, this pot is empty," he said.

And so it was. Pooh knew there was just one thing to do. He would have to fill it up again — and that meant climbing the honey tree.

The honey tree was a tall tree in the Hundred-Acre Wood with a beehive at the top. When Pooh and Piglet arrived there, Piglet looked at the hive nervously. He said in a small voice, "It certainly is a long way up."

Pooh hadn't remembered that the hive was in such a high place. But he saw that Piglet was right. Should he really go up there? he wondered.

Just then a swarm of bees buzzed out of the hive and into the woods. Another group followed them, and another. Watching the bees, Piglet said hopefully, "Maybe they're going to another honey tree — one that's a little lower."

"Yes," said Pooh, smiling. "Or perhaps to a honey bush, or a honey stream, or a honey lake."

Pooh, growing more excited by the minute, set out after the bees. Piglet hurried along behind. They followed the bees through the woods and over the bridge and into an open place. There the bees clustered around rows of brightly colored flowers.

It was Rabbit's garden.

"Hello, there," called Rabbit, who was working in the garden. "Would you like some of my buttercups?"

Pooh looked at the pretty yellow flowers. "They're very nice," he said. "But I was hoping for something more like . . . well, *honey* cups."

Piglet said, "Pooh, I don't think honey comes from flowers."

"Oh, but it does," said Rabbit, smiling. "Come here and I'll show you."

Rabbit knelt beside some pretty ruffled snapdragons.

"You see, Pooh," he said, "at the very bottom of flowers there's a sweet, sugary water called nectar. Bees love nectar the way you love honey."

Pooh smiled. Just thinking about honey gave him a warm glow.

Rabbit said, "The bee sucks the nectar from the flower with its tongue. Then the nectar goes into the bee's tummy and starts to turn to honey."

He offered Pooh the flowers he was holding.
"Maybe there is a bee in there right now!" exclaimed
Pooh.

But Rabbit just kept talking. "The bee brings the nectar back to the hive, and the other bees help finish turning it into honey," he said.

"That's very nice of them," said Pooh. "Do they do it just for bears?"

Rabbit chuckled and said, "No, Pooh. They do it for their babies. Baby bees eat honey, but whatever is left over can be eaten by Pooh bears and other animals."

Pooh was trying very hard to listen, but there was a rumbling in his tummy, and it was drowning out Rabbit's words.

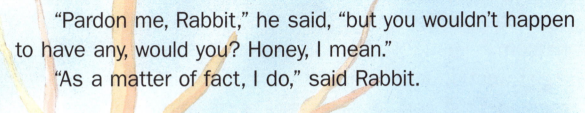

"Pardon me, Rabbit," he said, "but you wouldn't happen to have any, would you? Honey, I mean."

"As a matter of fact, I do," said Rabbit.

Rabbit brought out a bowl of honey for Pooh, some haycorn cakes for Piglet, and carrots for himself. After lunch, Piglet went off to help Rabbit in the garden. Pooh stretched out under the tree, thinking how he needed to get some honey for his late afternoon snack, which was only hours away.

"Think, think, think," he said to himself. As he tried to think, the sunshine beamed down, and his eyelids grew heavy.

Suddenly something was blocking the sun. Pooh opened his eyes, and there, towering overhead, was a giant snapdragon.

"Rabbit?" he called. "Piglet?" He looked around, but his

two friends were gone.

Pooh gazed up at the snapdragon and thought of the nectar inside. He could make it into honey, if only he were a bee.

Trying to be his most beelike self, Pooh started to buzz. It came out as more of a hum, and it went like this:

I am yellow and round, covered with fuzz,
Looking for dinner, all in a buzz.
I fly to the flowers, I hum a nice hum,
I sip up the nectar, yum, yum, yum!

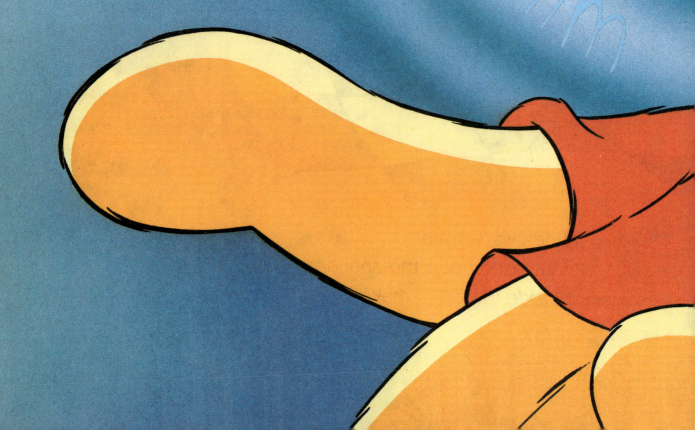

When Pooh finished his humming, he noticed a funny, fluttery feeling. Looking over his shoulder, he saw wings!

He was all fuzzy and covered with black and yellow
stripes.
Pooh Bear had turned into Pooh Bee!

Pooh looked at the snapdragon again. Suddenly he knew just what to do.

Spreading his wings, he flew into the air and buzzed around the flower. Why hadn't he noticed how sweet snapdragons smelled before? He took a deep breath, then landed on a petal.

Pooh explored the front of the snapdragon, then
crawled inside, deeper and deeper, until he came to a pool
of sugary nectar. Taking out a straw, he sucked up the
nectar into his special honey tummy.

Pooh was about to crawl back out when his nose began to itch. It itched, and it twitched, and it itched some more, until he let out a big sneeze.

Pooh opened his eyes. He was no longer Pooh Bee. He was Pooh Bear again.

"I hope you enjoyed your nap," said Piglet, who was standing beside him. "I picked these flowers for you while you were asleep."

"Thank you, Piglet," said Pooh, and he sneezed again.

It was getting late, so Pooh and Piglet said good-bye to Rabbit and headed home. Pooh still didn't have any honey, but he was already thinking of ways to get some.

He might float up to get it, with a balloon.

He might fly up to get it, with Owl.

He might bounce up to get it, with Tigger.

Or, if he was feeling sleepy, he might just take another nap, buzz back inside the giant snapdragon, and sip nectar all afternoon.

If he did, Pooh knew one thing for sure. He would have sweet dreams.